WRYB
&
the Race to the Melting Pot

~

by
Tom Ward,
Dodd I. Ferrelle, Bowen Craig

Bilbo Books Publishing
www.BilboBooks.com
bilbobookspublishing@gmail.com
(706)-549-1597

ISBN 979-8-9900028-2-1

Printed in the United States of America.
This is a work of fiction. Any resemblance of characters to
actual persons, living or dead, is purely coincidental.

Published in the United States of America by
Bilbo Books Publishing. Athens, Georgia, USA

Chapter 1

Two 15-year-old guys sprinted down the path beside the bank of the river. Each ran faster than he knew he was capable. They could not allow anyone to see them leaving the scene of what they had done. They slowed to cross a small stream, then began running again. The stream slowed them more than they had expected.

Suddenly, under the water, their shoes became heavy. Lifting their feet for each step became its own challenge. The crossing took about a minute but seemed far longer. When they stepped back onto dry land, the shoes remained heavy as each step brought a splash inside the shoe. Now, they felt even more hurried than before.

One was taller and had longer strides. The other one, kind of short, had to run harder to keep the pace as they continued alongside the riverbank. Once they had run around the next bend of the path, they stopped for a quick break. Both were out of breath. After a few moments of wheezing and breathing, one began to laugh. Then, the other joined in.

"That was a bad thing, bro," the shorter one said between deep breaths.

"Yep," the taller one replied.

"They'll know it was us," the short one declared.

"Of course they will, bro," the tall one agreed, "But they can't prove it."

The short one nodded. After finally catching his breath, he replied again. "Somebody might get hurt."

"Not my problem," the taller one answered. "Not your problem either." He watched the shorter one nod again in agreement, but it wasn't convincing.

"Doesn't matter now. It's done," the taller one added.

"Dude," the shorter one said, curiously, "Why are you standing in a hole?"

As the taller one glanced downward, he realized, in real time, that this had become the most terrifying moment of his life. Maybe it would be the last moment of his life.

"Bro, where are your feet?"

The taller one stared, in disbelief, at his feet, or at least where his feet should have been. They had disappeared into the ground.

"Is that...?"

"Yeah it is," the taller replied, his voice rising higher as the fear crept further into his heart. At the same time he was doing two things: trying not to panic...and...beginning to panic.

"It's quicksand," the shorter one replied. He could hear his own voice shaking, but he didn't want his friend to panic so he would try not to sound so shaky the next time he spoke. "I've seen it on YouTube. They say there's a lot of quicksand near this river. That's the real thing."

"Thanks, Sherlock. You don't have to tell me that it's real quicksand," the taller one fired back. Things were bad enough without his friend saying something dumb.

"Ok bro, just try not to panic 'cause you'll sink all the way in," the short one advised.

"Seriously, Sherlock? That's all you got? Don't sink all the way. Thanks bro. Now I know not to sink all the way in."

What a chump, the shorter one thought. He should just leave him in the quicksand if that was going to be the attitude. He pulled out his phone and checked the signal. None. He shook his head sideways to let his friend know there was no signal.

"I'll go for help. You can keep calm long enough for me to get back here in maybe ten minutes. Sound good?"

The taller one nodded. He agreed with the ten-minute time estimate, and he was pretty sure he would be fine for longer than that. Sounded like a good plan.

So the shorter one left, running as zealously as he had

from the scene of what they had done just a few minutes earlier. Except now it was much more urgent, and he was tired, and then he remembered that his shoes were soggy and heavy.

So the taller one just stood, wondering if this was the end, his friend having left for help. He stared again at the ground. It was really weird to see the ground but not your feet. He felt paralyzed. Helpless. He wondered if his friend could really get back in ten minutes. There was no way he could run that fast for long. The dude was still out of breath from running a few minutes ago.

Oh yeah, he thought, that thing a few minutes ago. He looked around and wondered if the quicksand was some type of divine punishment for what he had done a few minutes ago. Surely not. He hoped not. After all, it was just a little prank. No one would get hurt. Or would they?

On the bright side, if he lived through this quicksand, he would become a legend at school. People would stand in awe as he walked the halls between classes. Every single girl in the tenth grade would want to hear the story directly from him. And he would tell them. Every single one.

Then a sound startled him. Something was coming directly toward him through the dense trees and tall plants. As a reflex, he turned to run, but his legs would not move. Even worse, the struggle caused him to sink a few inches deeper into the quicksand. Great. That was all he needed.

All he could do was stand there, or sink, or float, or whatever he was doing. The sound grew louder and there was no doubt that the creature, whatever it was, would appear in a couple of seconds.

And then it happened. He could not believe his eyes.

The one thing in the world he least wanted to see had just appeared. Even in the middle of quicksand, his day had just gotten worse. Maybe this was some type of divine revenge for what he had just done. Maybe it was punishment for many things he had done. There were things, some bad things, that no one knew about except him.

But the reason didn't matter. All he could do was just stand there, or float there, or…why couldn't he figure out what he was doing in the quicksand? All he knew was that he could not move his legs, and when he saw the intruder, he knew he was sunk.

Literally, he knew he was sunk.

Chapter 2

Three days earlier

For the last several minutes, Taylor had wiped the drizzling mist of rain from his face several times. Now the rain fell harder, but he didn't dare wipe it from his eyes. Not now.

He kept his eyes focused on Keith, the leader of the pack of kids surrounding him. Well, almost surrounding him because a garbage dumpster sat behind him. But the other three sides were manned by Keith and his minions, the jerks who followed him around mindlessly. They let Keith do all of their thinking for them, and from the looks of everyone, probably their eating too.

Realizing he was about to get beaten up was a problem. It always was. Taylor had gained much experience at getting beaten up. But today was different. His parents were getting ready to take him on a cross-country trip, North and South, and if Taylor needed an Emergency Room trip that would become a problem. He decided to appeal to Keith's sense of fairness. He didn't look at anyone else. It was a way to appeal to Keith's oversized ego and also to insult the others by ignoring them.

"Guys, we're about to leave. It's vacation," Taylor began. "My mom will kill me if…"

Keith interrupted, as he typically did, to maintain his image of power and control. "She won't get the chance 'cause we're doing it right now."

Taylor slipped and fell on the muddy ground, causing the minions to laugh. No one noticed that he had fallen on purpose, or that he had grabbed a handful of mud.

Keith peered down at his prey. "You can't go crying to big brother and big sister now. They can't hear you from college. They probably can't remember you, you're so small."

The minions laughed. Of course they did.

Taylor smiled too, and they thought he was laughing with them, but he was laughing about the plan he would launch within the next minute.

"Seriously, guys. I need to go," Taylor said, once again focusing only on Keith, the leader.

Keith smiled. It was a bad smile, like the villain in a cheap movie. Then, he interrupted the smile to reply. "You will go…to the dumpster."

One of the minions grabbed Taylor's arm.

Then, Taylor smiled at Keith. It was the smile of someone who had just won. He looked past Keith, and as Keith began to turn to see what had distracted Taylor, the time had arrived for Taylor to yell.

"Mom!"

Everyone looked behind Keith.

At the same time, Taylor threw mud in the minion's

eyes, forcing him to let go of Taylor's arm while Taylor sprinted away. Keith and his minions chased him away from the dumpster and across the nearby basketball court. Taylor continued his sprint, grateful that he was easily the fastest kid in the neighborhood and maybe in his entire grade at school. He squeezed through a narrow gap in a backyard wooden fence that none of his pursuers could fit through. But he didn't slow down. He ran as fast as his swift legs would carry him.

Keith and the minions stopped at the backyard wooden fence. He pointed to his left. "Let's go this way. We might beat him to his house."

Keith yelled toward the fleeing Taylor, "You're still a Punk!"

Taylor heard the insult but pretended not to. He sure hated that word. It stung his soul to hear it.

~

Inside Taylor's home, his parents, Trevor and Vivian, gathered the final things for their long drive.

"Honey," Vivian asked as she zipped up a briefcase. "Do you think Taylor will remember to stay clean before our drive? He's been outside for a while."

"I'll put the over-under number at eighty percent," Trevor said with a grin.

She laughed. "Are those the odds of his staying clean?"

"Nope," he said, pretending to calculate the odds in his mind. "Eighty was the percentage of him that will be covered by mud."

Outside, Taylor sprinted toward the front door, trying to

get there before Keith and the others. He barely arrived at the front door first, but the door was locked. Taylor knocked frantically. Keith smiled as he and his friend sprinted to grab Taylor at the front door.

As the bullies arrived at the front steps, the door opened. There stood Taylor's Mom. She stared at Keith, making and keeping eye contact. She wanted the big bully to know that she knew. Somehow, she knew everything. Taylor smiled menacingly as he stepped into his home.

Taylor stepped inside, covered from head to toe in mud. He laughed, then they all laughed. Until that moment, he had wondered whether it was time for him to hear that he was officially grounded for the rest of his youthful years. His Mom spoke first. "So have you stayed clean like you promised?"

"Yes, I'm clean," he replied.

Now, his Dad joined in. "Would you like to check yourself in the mirror and try that answer again? It looks like you have a speck of mud…like…everywhere."

"I'm clean," he said boldly. "Mud baths are an alternative way of staying clean in some cultures."

"Name one," his Dad said with a smile.

"The ancient Egyptians."

"Go grab a shower," his Dad said, shaking his head and still grinning.

When Taylor had left the room, Trevor glanced at Vivian. "This bullying has to stop, and Keith's parents refuse to believe he is a bully."

"When we come back," she said firmly, "We might just have to fight fire with fire."

"Us bullying the kids?" Trevor was surprised and hoped she had mispoken.

"You'll see," she said seriously. "We'll fight back when we get back from the trip."

The gray mid-size SUV sped down Interstate 55 South from Chicago. Taylor, a freshman in high school, or at least he would soon be a freshman, observed that everything about this day seemed to be gray. His family's SUV was gray. The vehicle's interior was gray. His sweatshirt was gray. The sky was gray. Even both of his parents, whose heads he observed from his place in the backseat, were turning grayer each year. That was fitting on this day in which they traveled southward from Chicago because life itself seemed to be kind of gray. Let's pause here, he thought, and go back and add up the gray. On this foggy morning, even the air itself was gray. His neighborhood was gray, at least gray and gloomy because Taylor happened to be the smallest kid in the neighborhood, and that meant he got bullied.

For most of his life, that had never been a problem because his older brother and sister would stick up for him. Two years ago, his big brother left for college, and this summer, just a few weeks ago, his older sister left for the state university, so now it was just him and now there was no one to protect him. Getting pushed or shoved or sometimes even hit was not his idea of fun, but it seemed to be the reality, the new reality of his neighborhood. It was even worse at school. Why was it just because someone was born shorter and skinnier than everybody else, people felt the need to attack him? It seemed kind of barbaric to Taylor, but that was life. At least it was his life.

School was even worse than home because of the Cools and the Punks. It was like the entire school was either a Cool or a Punk. Taylor knew he hadn't done anything bad to be put in the Punks, but somehow, that became his label. Or maybe it was just that he wasn't a Cool, so everybody left over became one of the Punks. But why? He liked the same music as the Cools, and he rooted for the same teams. Many of the Cools had been his friends all through elementary and middle school. Some of them had come over to hang out when Taylor's brother came home from college. The kids were riveted as his big bro told all about college football games and how beautiful the college girls were. To kids his age, it sounded like paradise.

But now? Somehow, Taylor being labeled a Punk had changed everything. There was no more hanging out. They still wanted to watch ball games, but Taylor was no longer invited. They would still speak to him in the halls between classes, unless other Cools were around. Then, not a chance.

Taylor needed to tell somebody about the Cools and Punks. He called his big brother, Mark, who replied that it was the dumbest thing he had ever heard. Mark explained that high school kids do goofy stuff because everyone is so desperate to fit in. It will all pass.

That's great, Taylor thought, but he hadn't even started high school yet, and he was already a social outcast. That could haunt him for the rest of his life.

He wondered if it would end up on his permanent record. He could just see it now…nice kid…good grades… but he's a Punk.

The movement ahead caught his eye, and he noticed that his Mom was talking to him again. He removed the earbuds and learned from her that they were passing through St. Louis. He glanced up from his phone to see the Arch. Pretty cool.

And then there was the Mississippi River. That reminded him of Aunt Flossie, but he wasn't sure why. She told the best stories, out there on her front porch as the sun set. At least that's what his brother and sister always said. As he looked back at his phone, Taylor realized that he hadn't listened to Aunt Flossie's stories about the mysterious part of the world they call the Mississippi Delta.

His brother and sister had listened and loved every moment of it. Even this week, before the trip, they had both told him they wished they could make the trip to see Aunt Flossie and hear those cool stories.

That figures. They had loved the stories and he had been too busy watching the lightning bugs and listening to the crickets. Now that he really thought about it, he had watched and listened to just about everything there except Aunt Flossie and her stories.

He hated that. It was just one more thing that his brother and sister did better than he did. His brother and sister always did things the right way, and then there was Taylor. The other kid. Maybe, he thought, Aunt Flossie might not mind telling some of those stories again. Maybe he was old enough now to pay attention. Maybe he would find out what was so different about this part of the world. Maybe he could tell some of the stories and the Cools would pay attention. Maybe he could become a Cool if they cared about what he had to say.

He couldn't decide which was worse, school or the neighborhood. Kids in the neighborhood had somehow found out how good his grades were and they made fun of him and pushed him and shoved him and hit him even more, but he couldn't make bad grades. That would ruin his opportunity to go to college and get out of the neighborhood.

Plus things weren't always great at home. Ever since that pandemic a couple of years ago, Mom and Dad's business just wasn't what it used to be. Even their hair, each of their heads of hair, got gray quickly. It was hard not to see that gray hair and think about the pandemic and the stress and college tuition for two kids and those late night chats in hushed voices so the only child still at home wouldn't hear.

So his home was bad. School was bad. The neighborhood was bad. Everything was bad. What Taylor needed was a refuge.

He hoped this place in Mississippi would be exactly that for him, a refuge. His Great Aunt Flossie had outlived his grandparents, whom he still missed really badly. It was always great to see Flossie because she was sweet and welcoming and seemed to understand him. Plus, she looked just like his grandfather, and that always made him feel better. When he saw her, it was like Flossie was a link between ancient history and modern times. She had actually lived through stuff that doesn't even seem real these days. Like the Second World War. Taylor needed a refuge and it seemed like Mississippi might be exactly that, and maybe Aunt Flossie would be as well.

Taylor could not even remember the name of the town Flossie lived in. All they remembered was it was where Aunt Flossie lived and it was in Mississippi, so when they went, they only called it Aunt Flossie's house in Mississippi. So much had changed since the last trip to Aunt Flossie's house. The family had not been down there since the pandemic. That took basically two years out of their travel time, and then between his older brother and his older sister going to college, well, they just haven't been able to go for the last couple of years. But here they were, finally returning to a town known only to him as Aunt Flossie's house in Mississippi.

Over the music, in his earbuds, he faintly heard a voice that probably belonged to his Mom, so he took out the earbuds and asked what she said.

She turned her face around to see him, smiled happily and said: "Only nine hours until we make it to Refuge."

Did Mom just say Refuge?

"Mom, what did you just say?"

She smiled, as she always does. "We'll make it to Refuge in about nine hours."

"Where is Refuge?"

"Oh," she said. "That's where Aunt Flossie lives."

Taylor was surprised, especially since he had just thought of that word: refuge. "I thought Aunt Flossie lived in Green-something Mississippi."

"Refuge is close to Greenville. We called it Greenville when you were little so you could find it on that Triple-A Road Atlas you loved to look at during long drives."

Taylor hadn't thought about that Triple-A Road Atlas in years. When he was a little kid, that oversized map was as big as he was. Maybe he was older than he felt, if his childhood memories seemed so distant.

Maybe this was a sign of great things to come. He had just thought that he needed a refuge from school, the neighborhood, and his stressed-out parents. Then, a few minutes later, his Mom said that they would be in Refuge in nine hours. Yes, it was definitely a good sign.

~

As the gray vehicle sped southward, Taylor became lost in his thoughts. He was a high schooler now, at least he would be in a few weeks when school began. He was a different person than the little kid who last visited Aunt Flossie's home as a fifth grader. His mind and body had grown. Well, at least his mind had grown. He was still as short and skinny as always. Still, Taylor knew he had changed. He was no longer just the kid who tagged along behind his brother and sister. He no longer had to yell or spill something to be noticed.

And then there was Aunt Flossie. As much as he had changed, he hoped she hadn't changed at all. He hoped she still had that water hose in the front yard that the kids all drank from while playing outside. He hoped the days were still so hot and humid that you had to swim through the air instead of walking through it. He hoped she still had those two swings on her front porch.

He wondered why the homes in his own neighborhood didn't have swings on front porches. As he considered this, he realized that the homes didn't have front porches at all. Why not? Maybe that was why most of the people in his subdivision didn't know each other. Maybe everyone was too busy anyway. Or maybe they thought they were too busy. Or maybe they just pretended.

Taylor decided that he liked the world of front porches better than back porches. Front porches made people nicer, more aware of their neighbors. And maybe it helped with bullying too, when adults actually sat on the front porches and knew what their kids were doing.

Chapter 3

The smile lit up her hazel-brown eyes.

At that moment, the world changed.

Until then, Taylor doubted that he would ever see Aunt Flossie again. Sure, she was sitting there on her front porch with him, but he hadn't thought it was the real Aunt Flossie. He understood that it sometimes happens to older people. Maybe they're mostly there, but not completely there. But in that moment, he realized that he was now with the true, authentic, storytelling Aunt Flossie.

Taylor could read people's eyes. It was a gift. He had never told anyone that before, because it sounds like a dumb thing for a teenager to say. Especially a guy. But he knew he could understand almost anyone through their eyes.

They had first arrived at Aunt Flossie's, maybe half an hour before sunset. Everyone hugged and said they missed each other. Aunt Flossie stepped back and admired how much Taylor had begun to look like a young man now that he was about to start high school. All of that was sincere, but there was something else in those hazel eyes that they shared. Actually, their entire family had those eyes, and it complimented their black hair. But Flossie's eyes spoke in ways that others did not.

In those first moments, he saw uncertainty in those ancient eyes, but why? Was she uncertain of her own memory, of her recollections of Taylor and his older siblings? Was she just pretending to remember him? There were so many possibilities, and most of them were pretty bad. But then the smile came, and Taylor could read that too.

The smile came when his parents said they would go change clothes and maybe grab a quick nap before the four of them would be enjoying a late dinner. Flossie had made gumbo, and the cornbread was ready to go in the oven, so they could eat any time. That was when Taylor asked if Flossie would sit on the porch and watch the sunset together, like he and his siblings used to do with her.

That was when she smiled. Not a regular smile, although those are great, but a joyous, contagious smile. It was the smile of someone who longed to connect with Taylor and had just realized that the connection had never left.

That was the moment when he understood her uncertainty. She wasn't uncertain about herself or her memory. Instead, she wasn't sure whether this little kid, now a teenager, would still appreciate her and want to spend time with her.

Most people just called him names or tried to stuff him into neighborhood trash cans, so someone hoping to hang with him was pretty cool.

The colors were brilliant, as good or greater than a beach sunset. For the first few minutes, each of them admired the sunset without a word. Taylor did things like that all the time, but that was because they were all on their phones. Silence without phones was, well, different.

"Sunsets are different in the Delta," she said, softly, still gazing out at the evening horizon.

"Why is that?"

"A lot of things are different here."

"Aunt Flossie, sorry to ask this, but I don't really understand what the Mississippi Delta is. Like, what is it? And why do people keep saying things are so different here? And where does it start and end?"

"Child, the Delta starts in a state park in northern Minnesota."

If anyone but Aunt Flossie called him a child, he would deliver a spirited rebuttal and probably get grounded for a week. But Aunt Flossie, well, that was just how she talked. She called everyone a child, even Taylor's parents. Probably his grandparents too.

"Ok, I'll bite," Taylor replied with a laugh. "How does

the Mississippi Delta start at a state park in northern Minnesota?"

"Child, it's called Lake Itasca, and the lake becomes a stream, and that stream begins flowing northward toward Canada."

"Canada?"

"That's right, child. By then it's officially the Mississippi River. Thankfully, in Minnesota that water turns and heads southward. By the time it reaches St. Louis, it has been joined by eighteen different rivers."

"Wish I was that popular," Taylor said with a smile.

"Sure is great to see you smile," Aunt Flossie replied.

Taylor nodded, wondering how his face usually looked these days.

Aunt Flossie continued. "But just before it reaches St. Louis, two more rivers come crashing in to join the party."

"Which two rivers, Aunt Flossie?" Taylor asked.

"The Ohio River and the Allegheny River. That's when the last leg of the journey begins."

"So how long is the last leg of the river?"

"'Bout a thousand miles."

"That's a pretty big last leg," he said with a laugh.

"That's the Mississippi River that's so famous, when it's that big. That's why they call it the Mighty, Muddy, Mississippi."

"So why is it so muddy?"

"Child, you are becoming a man. You never would have asked a great question like that a few years ago."

Taylor smiled. Aunt Flossie understood how to build people up, even as she told a great story.

"It's the snow," she replied, nodding to his question with even more approval. "Round here, a big winter storm becomes part of history. Back in ninety-three, we got a bazillion inches of snow. In two thousand and twenty four, the whole South froze up so hard it could have broken into little pieces."

Taylor laughed.

"But up North, they get snow all the time. So in the springtime, the snow melts and flows into streams and it carries good soil into those creeks and rivers. Then they empty into the Mississippi."

"That's a lot of water at the same time," Taylor said as he thought about it. "Is it ever too much water?"

Flossie nodded. "Now, you're really thinking, child. 'Bout a hundred years ago, there were entire towns swept away by the floods. There was standing water thirty feet deep in some places. Entire counties were under water."

Taylor could hardly believe it. "Do you ever worry about that happening again?"

"Nope," she replied, shaking her head confidently. "The government engineers take care of that with a lot of technology and levees and stuff. That's why nobody lives right on the river anymore."

Finally, Taylor was beginning to understand why his older brother and sister loved listening to Aunt Flossie. If she told the story of how to make a peanut butter sandwich, Taylor would sit in awe to see how it ended.

That he heard his parents approaching.

"How was the sunset?" his Dad asked.

"Colorful," Aunt Flossie replied.

"It's gumbo time," his Dad added.

Aunt Flossie thanked them both, and they all went inside to finish preparing dinner. It seemed like his parents were always doing nice, considerate things. So thoughtful. And they were happy to see him and Aunt Flossie catching up. Plus, they had to be soooo happy to see him go so long without looking at his phone.

~

Dinner was of course delicious. Taylor devoured the gumbo and the cornbread, on which he spread plenty of butter. Everybody praised both, and Flossie just nodded thanks. Her nod, Taylor thought, said thank you but also said that she knew her gumbo and cornbread were great.

Flossie explained that the entire human race could be explained by gumbo. That seized Taylor's attention. She explained that most people had their own gumbo recipe, and that was the entire point. You used what you had. Even for Flossie, the gumbo might differ from year to year based on which local crops had the best harvests. And for humans, each community should be like a big ol' pot of gumbo. Every person is different, but we should blend together to become the best we can be.

Just when Taylor thought he couldn't eat another bite of anything, Flossie revealed her signature dessert, Mississippi Mud Pie. He hadn't thought about that in a few years, but when Flossie brought it out, he had to get a heaping helping.

"Child, I haven't seen anybody eat like that since the last time you were here." Everybody laughed.

Everyone helped clean the kitchen after dinner. Then, Taylor's Mom and Dad went into the den to watch a movie. They were taking full advantage of the opportunity to hang out together while Taylor finally had time with Aunt Flossie, unencumbered by his older siblings or other distractions.

They filled their glasses with sweet tea. Taylor put a lemon slice in his and Flossie did the same but with lime. It was time for his questions to resume.

"So what's so different about the Mississippi Delta?"

Flossie once again nodded with approval. "Sometimes, child, the river just moves. Like, it's there one day and then the next day it has changed its path."

Taylor was surprised. "That's kind of scary."

"Yes indeed," she said with a laugh. "Back in the eighties, the eighteen eighties, Vicksburg was one of the most important river cities in America. One morning they woke up and the river was gone. Done, child. No more."

This was too strange to be true. "So what did they do?"

"It took the US government 'bout twenty years to move the path of the river back to Vicksburg. Finally got it done. Business really dried up for a while until the river came back."

Taylor smiled at her joke and nodded. She was pleased that he hadn't missed it.

Aunt Flossie took a sip of her sweet tea. Taylor had almost forgotten it was in her hand. Then he remembered that he had his own glass of sweet tea too.

Then, she continued. "So for thousands of years, they think, the Mississippi Delta was underwater. It was the floor of the river. All that soil coming from up North ended up on the riverbed."

Now he got it. "So the next time the river changed its path, there was all of this flat land with great soil?" Taylor said.

Flossie's grin broadened as he spoke. "So when the settlers discovered Mississippi, they also found all this flat land with rich soil. It was a farmer's paradise. But then came the greed."

Taylor noticed that her face became serious. He had to ask. "What greed?"

"It wasn't enough to make a lot of money. They wanted to capture other human beings and force them to farm the land for free."

Taylor nodded. In that moment, he understood a lot about the past that had never really made sense. He was counting the days until his American History class started. He would tell this story in class, and everybody would know about it. Maybe somebody would livestream it. If the popular girls learned who he was, he might become one of the Cools instead of a Punk. That raised the question of how someone could move from the Punks to the Cools. Would that be the transfer portal?

Aunt Flossie waited. Taylor realized that she was watching him consider what he had just learned. This wasn't just her story. It was their story, together. She was the storyteller and he was the audience.

When he glanced back at her, she nodded and took a long sip of that sweet tea. Then, she continued.

"So these people were working on farms and plantations," she said. "They had brought their music with them, and they sang their songs. But as the years went by, they sang their own songs, about their families and their sad, sad lives."

"Got it," Taylor said with a grin. "The blues."

Flossie smiled again. "That's right. Then people took the blues and created jazz, and then they created rock-n-roll. Everything comes from the blues, and the blues come from the Delta."

Taylor sipped on his tea and had another question. "So the jazz in New Orleans, and the rock-n-roll in Memphis, all of that comes from the blues in the Delta?"

"Think about it," she answered, "What do New Orleans, St. Louis and Memphis have in common?"

He smiled. "They're all on the Mississippi River."

"Bingo," she replied. "So when slaves were sold at these slave auctions in big cities, they took their music with them."

Taylor tried to imagine the life of a slave. What would it be like to have no freedom, to never decide to go fishing or play ball just because you want to? And college? Not a chance. What about being separated from your family, or never having a single front-porch conversation with your great aunt because someone else owned the front porch? Suddenly, the question of being one of the Cools or Punks at school didn't seem so big.

"And there's one more thing," Flossie added. The tone of her voice sounded different, and Taylor took a sip of his sweet tea and sneaked a peek at her facial expression over the top of his glass.

"What's that?" Taylor asked, trying not to reveal his surprise and possible concern.

"A lot of magical stuff happens in the Delta. Strange stuff."

He was riveted. "What kind of stuff?"

"All kinds of stuff," Flossie replied seriously. "Some people see things, and they see people who shouldn't be there. And maybe they aren't there at all. Nobody knows for sure."

"Okay," Taylor muttered, unsure of how to reply. He tried to think of something better to say. Finally, he had something, though it wasn't very good. "Has anyone in our family had strange things happen?"

Flossie smiled. "Some people have seen things down by the river. People or spirits or something. But then a lot of people have seen things like that. And then there was Cousin Freddy who kept getting hit by lightning."

Taylor laughed, and then wondered whether he should be laughing at a family member struck by lightning even once, much less more than once. "What happened to Cousin Freddy?"

"Well, Cousin Freddy was serving in the Great War, do you know what that was?"

Taylor nodded. "The First World War."

"Exactly," Flossie said with a nod of approval. "Cousin Freddy was riding a horse and got struck by lightning. Knocked him clean off the horse and left him paralyzed from the waist down."

"That's awful," Taylor said. "Poor Cousin Freddy."

"Kind of," she replied, which surprised Taylor. "They said Freddy could see the future after that lightning got him, and a lot people paid a lot of money to get their futures told or to get advice from Freddy. And they say he told Old Man Beasley to get out of the stock market right before the crash of '29."

"Wow," answered an impressed Taylor.

"Freddy loved sports, but the only sport he could enjoy without using his legs was fishing. So he fished a lot. One day, some of his friends took him fishing. They were getting out of the boat because a storm was coming. They sat Freddy under a tree while they packed up everything, but then lightning hit the tree and blew Freddy up in the air, just like the first lightning did."

Taylor just shook his head. "Did it kill him?"

"Nope, the second lightning didn't kill him either. Strange enough, he got his legs back from the second lightning bolt. He would walk again."

"Is it ok if I laugh?" Taylor asked.

Flossie nodded, but Taylor got the impression that the story wasn't over.

"The third strike was strange," she said.

Taylor wondered how anything could be stranger than the first two.

"Since the second lightning strike, Freddy walked long distances every day because he was just so happy he could walk. But one day, on one of his long walks, a quick storm came up…"

Taylor laughed. "There's no way…"

"Yes indeed," Flossie said with a smile. "A third lightning bolt got him, and he was lucky to survive. But he was paralyzed again."

"You call that lucky?" Taylor asked with a laugh.

"Was he unlucky to get hit by lightning that many times, or was he lucky to survive?"

"Good question," Taylor asked.

"And then there was the fourth one," Flossie added.

Taylor shook his head again, this time too into the story to comment.

"Cousin Freddy passed away," she explained. "After some time, a storm came up, and a big ol' bolt of lightning came down and busted up his tombstone. It's kind of still together, but it has two large cracks where the lightning got it."

Taylor laughed freely now. "Anything else?"

"There's more than you can imagine or understand," she said, once again seriously. "But beware of those foggy places on the slews from the river. And beware the quicksand."

"Quicksand?" Taylor said with a laugh. Suddenly, he began to doubt whether all of this mysterious Delta stuff was real. "Quicksand in Mississippi?"

"Oh yes indeed," she replied. "My neighbor got in some last week while he and his brothers were hunting."

"Was his life in danger?" Taylor asked.

"Not then, but the more he tells the story, the more dangerous it got. I'm afraid he'll get carried away and say it killed him the next time he tells it."

They laughed.

"So be careful to study what you see and hear, especially down near the river. The Mississippi River is Muddy and Mighty, but it's also Mysterious."

"Got it," Taylor replied as he memorized every detail of the story. This would absolutely help him meet girls at some point in the future. It might even get him into the Cools.

Chapter 4

Taylor woke to the delicious aroma of the breakfast Flossie was preparing downstairs in the kitchen. It was going to be a classic day, he could tell. Last night Flossie had mentioned the annual Melting Pot Festival the next day and everyone agreed to make the trip. Flossie had even prepared an extra pot of gumbo to enter into the festival's annual gumbo contest. She said she hadn't participated in many years, but since Taylor and his folks happened to be visiting on the weekend of the festival, she would join in the fun.

Taylor stretched his arms and then sprang out of bed, ready for the day. That day would begin with one of Flossie's great breakfasts, which Taylor had enjoyed since childhood. Except the grits, which he had steadfastly refused to try. His siblings made fun of him for years for refusing to at least try the well-known Southern delicacy, but they were gross. Of that, he was certain. He figured this morning that avoiding the grits wouldn't hurt Aunt Flossie's feelings since she expected it. They all had expected it.

"Got a surprise for you this morning," Aunt Flossie said. 'It's a breakfast dish from another country."

Taylor was feeling pretty adult-ish this morning, so he decided to give it a try. "Where's it from?"

"It was created in South America by the Muskogee tribe way back in the 1500s," Flossie explained. "It's extremely popular in Malaysia. And one state in America, South Carolina, even has laws on how it can be packaged for sale."

Taylor laughed. "Is this a dish or a drug? Did you smuggle it in from Columbia?"

Everybody laughed.

"So what is the name of this exotic international dish?" Taylor asked.

"We'll tell you after you try it."

As Flossie placed it in a bowl beside his plate, she and his parents watched closely.

Taylor looked around and laughed. "There's no need to stare at me."

"But we want to," his Dad replied with a smile.

"Should I put anything in it?" Taylor asked as he eyed the dish suspiciously.

"Maybe butter, or a dash of black pepper," his Dad replied.

Taylor took a bite. "Actually, this is good," he said before taking another bite. "So what do we call this ancient

Muskogee food?"

"Grits," Flossie said with a smile, as his parents began to applaud.

Taylor smiled, knowing this would become one of the family stories repeated forever. He was kind of glad, because not many of the family stories focused on him.

~

They drove into the park and campgrounds, passing under a baby-blue sign that read, in large navy blue letters: WELCOME TO THE 44TH ANNUAL MELTING POT FESTIVAL.

Taylor hadn't known what to expect, but it was a sizable crowd. That made sense, the park was just one turn off of the U.S. Highway that crossed the Mighty Mississippi River from Refuge, Mississippi to Shives, Arkansas. And with the casino nearby, plenty of people saw the signs back on the highway before the turnoff. Flossie said the festival was a pretty big deal each year.

They found a parking space and walked toward the crowd. Taylor's Dad carried the pot of hot gumbo, both of his hands covered with oven mitts.

The festival had started early in the morning with events like the three-legged race, the corn hole tournament, the stick-horse race for kids, and the checkers tournament. They arrived later, a little early for the two events that mattered most to them. The entire family would cheer on Aunt Flossie in the Melting Pot Festival Gumbo Contest, and they would cheer on Taylor as he ran in the Race to the Melting Pot.

At the same time, the food contests kicked off with the J & J championship featuring the best jams and jellies in the Delta. Then there was the contest that always baffles non-Delta people, the fried catfish-and-spaghetti cookoff. No one in Mississippi has ever publicly claimed to know anyone who prepared fried catfish and spaghetti other than those who are connected somehow to the Delta.

So, with the other races concluded and blue ribbons awarded for great cooking, the festival had come down to the premier events, the gumbo contest and the race.

Between the parking area and the festival entrance sat an old bait shop that looked like it had been there since the dawn of time. The straightest path to the festival went just a few feet from the bait shop, so Taylor was close enough to catch every detail for the stories he would tell back home. The building was made of old concrete blocks covered by a tin roof with plenty of rust stains. The front door was covered with small posters and post cards with advertisements for soft drinks, fishing lures, and chocolate snacks. Taylor guessed that most of them, except for the soda, were no longer made.

In front of the bait shop sat an ancient wooden bench that Taylor guessed was every bit as old as the store itself.

It was occupied at that moment by two older men who seemed not to have a care in the world. He noticed one of them apparently speaking, followed by the other one laughing. He wondered how much time would pass before either left that bench.

To his surprise, at that moment, both men sprang up onto their feet and sported their best smiles. Taylor glanced around to see what had brought them to their feet, but then realized it was Aunt Flossie.

"Morning, Miss Flossie," they both said, almost in unison.

"Morning, Mister Clovis. Morning, Mister Jackson," she said in reply while returning the smile.

These men were wowed by Aunt Flossie. In a moment, Taylor realized that she was much more than the delicious-food-cooking, story-telling great aunt. She was a big deal on the social scene in Refuge, Mississippi.

The better he got to know Flossie, he realized, the more complex and impressive she became.

"You've got a nice-looking family," Clovis said.

Jackson looked directly at Taylor. "Son, don't believe a word she says about me."

Flirting is flirting, in any age or language, Taylor thought. He nodded and laughed at Jackson and nodded a thanks to Clovis for the compliment.

Taylor scanned the scene, looking for teenagers. He had read online about the Race to the Melting Pot, a part-footrace and part-obstacle course through the park and near the riverbanks. He might be short and skinny, and not all that good with girls, but he could run. Maybe winning the festival race would also give him a story for the girls back home.

Someone, maybe a local leader, announced the beginning of the festival. She introduced the judges of the gumbo contest. Aunt Flossie had said that the festival committee chooses the judges, a big honor in this area. Each stood and received applause: an insurance agent, the owner of a storage-unit place with a clever name, and the general manager of the nearby casino. The casino sat near the river and employed many of the people in Refuge and Greenville.

Then the lady introduced another lady, the head of the historical society, who explained the background of the Melting Pot Festival. It seems that the people of Refuge weren't getting along that well with the people from nearby Greenville, who also didn't get along with the people in Shives, Arkansas, right across the Mississippi River from Refuge. The festival was designed to get everyone to play nice together, as Taylor's kindergarten teacher liked to say. They used the title Melting Pot to celebrate the melting-pot culture of people from different backgrounds, and also to represent the big pots of gumbo that were entered in the gumbo contest each year.

Taylor glanced around again and spotted two dudes who might become his friends. One was taller and pretty athletic, and his friend was about Taylor's height but with a much thicker frame. He decided to be confident, because no one here would call him a Punk. No one here would make fun of him. Today was like a brand new beginning, kind of like college would be in a few years.

He walked over to the two of them. "Guys, I'm…"

"Short," the tall guy said, finishing Taylor's sentence for him. "You're short. Is that your name too?"

Both the guys laughed, including the shorter one, whom Taylor was pretty sure was the shortest of the three of them.

Taylor just looked at him without responding. How could this be happening to him again? Did the Cools back home find out about this trip and notify the Cools in Mississippi to make fun of him?

He decided to ignore the remark. "I'm Taylor and I came over from Refuge, and I…"

The tall guy interrupted again. "Refuge? You're from Refuge? I guess that makes you a refugee."

Both the guys laughed again.

"Hey refugee," the tall kid called out.

"Yeah?" Taylor replied, and immediately knew he

should have already walked away.

"Wherever you go to school, what do the cool kids call you?"

They both laughed once again. Taylor felt as if he had been kicked in the stomach. Did he have some big scarlet letter on his forehead? Can people somehow sense that he doesn't fit in at school? Do they somehow know that he doesn't fit in anywhere else either?

Taylor turned and walked back toward his family. What was it about him that invited people to abuse him? Maybe he should ask his Mom to home-school him, and while they were at it, to move to another neighborhood. That wasn't asking too much, was it?

Taylor knew his face betrayed everything he was thinking when he noticed that his Dad had watched him walk from the two jerks back over to the family. His Dad didn't mention Taylor's dejected look, but surprised him by changing the subject from the unspoken pain.

"Taylor, some of Aunt Flossie's friends are here, and they have a son your age."

Taylor was introduced to Lem, from a Lebanese family who lived in the area. Lem appeared physically fit, at least enough to perform well in the Race to the Melting Pot. They chatted for a few minutes, then walked toward the starting point after hearing the announcement that the race would soon begin.

"Looks like we have two refugees,"the short guy said, "Hey Lem, who is this little child you are babysitting?"

Lem and Taylor ignored him.

The taller one laughed. "Well guys, I hope you like the look of our rear ends. 'Cause that will be your view when we cross the finish line."

"Not sure about that," the short one replied. "If Lem is a Kenyan, we might be in trouble. Those Kenyans run all the time instead of eating. The rays of the Sun are their food."

The taller one laughed. "He looks Middle Eastern or Central American to me. Hope he's not a terrorist."

Taylor grinned. Lem caught on and grinned back. They walked off, leaving the two bullies wondering why they weren't in on the joke.

"Go!" the casino manager called out over the PA system, and all the young people and the young at heart, as the flyer described them, sprinted across the open field that served as the first leg of the race.

Interestingly, most of the people were elementary school kids and their parents. The only four teenagers Taylor saw were himself, Lem, and the two jerks. He didn't notice any college students. So it wasn't surprising that the four of them sprinted immediately out to the front of the pack, leaving everyone else behind.

To Taylor's surprise, the other short guy was keeping up with them. So the four of them ran together, fiercely but together, at least until they encountered the obstacles. That would separate the athletes from the pretenders, he thought. He was also surprised that everyone except the four of them seemed to consider the race as some type of fun run. For the teenagers, this was much different. It was fierce. It was ugly. It was just like a day in high school.

That was when he heard the yell.

His feet stopped abruptly when he realized that the yell had come from his new friend Lem. It wasn't a scream. It didn't come from fear. It sounded like pain.

He turned around to see Lem trying to get back up after falling. The tall and short guys did a running half-turn and then sped up again after seeing what had happened.

Taylor hated to stop, but he had to check on Lem.

"Stepped in a hole," Lem said. "I'm fine. Catch those guys."

Taylor helped him stand and take a step or two, and then nodded and sprinted back into the race. About a hundred yards ahead lay the thick woods where some of the obstacles were placed. The tall and short guys were at that moment disappearing into those woods.

"You can't let them win," Lem said.

"I know."

"Can you run fast?" Lem asked, hopeful for a good answer.

Taylor nodded and grinned. "Like the wind."

"Stop," the tall kid called out. The short kid, as always, did what he said.

"Help me with this," the tall one said, as he approached the sign with the arrow pointing the runners along the right path straight ahead. They quickly turned the sign so the arrow would point to a smaller, less-cleared path to the right.

"That should take care of our victory in this race," he said with a laugh. "He's not from around here. Everybody else will know the sign is wrong and they'll take the right path."

They ran hard, to be out of sight by the time Taylor arrived at the sign. Because misdirecting Taylor wasn't enough, they took an additional shortcut near the riverbank so they wouldn't have to run so hard.

That was where the quicksand awaited them.

Chapter 5

Taylor wanted to slow as he approached the dark woods, but the lady at the festival's opening said the path would be well marked. Plus, the two chumps ahead of him had run into the woods at full speed, so if he was going to catch them, he would do the same.

About twenty yards in, he saw the sign directing runners to the right. The path straight ahead seemed like the easier and maybe even safer route, but he didn't have time to check his phone's GPS. In fact, he realized that he hadn't checked his phone all day.

He continued his sprint, running not to catch those guys but to beat them.

And then he stopped.

In almost the blink of an eye, he had run into a fog. He knew he had to be near the river, because this much fog, or steam, or whatever it was could only come from a lot of water. He could barely see.

He took a deep breath after sprinting into the woods, but the air was so hot and steamy that it was hard to breathe in. It didn't seem possible that the shaded woods could be hotter than the sun-baked open fields, but that was exactly what was happening.

Then there were the sounds. He noticed more bird sounds, maybe the sounds of large birds, than he had ever heard in the Mississippi Delta.

The best path, he realized, was the path itself. So he decided to take a slow jog and keep his feet moving to get out of this weird stuff as quickly as possible. He decided that this wouldn't be much fun for the parents and young kids participating in the run. It sure wasn't much fun for him right now.

When he turned to glance around, he lost his feel for the right direction. He did a complete-360, hoping something would look familiar, but nothing did.

He turned another circle and noticed a form that could not be what it appeared. It was a figure, it was maybe a rock shape that looked like someone. Against his better judgment, he stepped closer. It was a person, sitting on a large rock on the riverbank. The river, or maybe it was a slew from the river, was barely visible. There was some stick in the air, or a small tree. No, he realized that it was an old-fashioned cane fishing pole. Somebody was actually sitting in this dense fog on the riverbank, fishing in the slew.

It was time to run.

Until he heard the voice.

"Good day for fishin'," the voice said.

Taylor decided that, even though this was really creepy, he couldn't be rude and run off. Plus, maybe the guy could help him get back on the path. Actually, that was the real reason Taylor wasn't running off.

"Yeah," Taylor called out. "Looks like a great day for fishing."

"It's always a great day for fishin'," the man replied.

His voice sounded old, or maybe just kind of old, but Taylor couldn't see his face clearly in the fog.

"Sir, do you know where we are?" Taylor asked, immediately regretting the dumb question. He tried to overcome it. "There's supposed to be a lot of people running through here in a minute."

"Naw," the man answered. "It's jes' us."

The man's utter confidence was contagious, Taylor thought. He felt confident approaching the man.

"Hadn't thought about that, that it's always a good day for fishing," Taylor replied.

"Do you know why?" The man asked.

"Nope," Taylor said honestly.

"It's always a great day to do what you love. It's always a great day when you do what you want to do the most."

"Makes sense," Taylor responded. A moment ago, all he wanted was to run through this fog and forget all about it. But now, he was glad for this detour and someone who just might become his newest friend.

"I'm Taylor," he said.

"They call me a lot of different names," the man replied. "You can call me WRYB."

"Well good morning, WRYB," Taylor answered. "What kind of fishing do you do?"

"I'm a flaw fisherman," the mysterious figure replied.

Taylor wondered if the mysterious figure had said fly fisherman or flaw fisherman. "Did you say fly fisherman?"

Through the fog, Taylor saw WRYB's head nodding, as he began to reply. "In yo' heart, ya know."

"Well, I'm glad you're doing what you really want to do today," Taylor responded, while wondering what a flaw fisherman caught or tried to catch.

"So what do you want to do today?" WRYB asked.

Taylor thought about it. There were many things he wanted today. He wanted to win the race. He wanted to defeat those two chumps, the tall one and the short one. He wanted kids his own age to think he was cool. He wanted to have confidence with girls. He wanted to not be so short or skinny. He wanted real friends. He wanted to not feel so bad about himself.

Taylor had never told anyone all of that, and a stranger would not be the first to hear it. So he answered by talking about the race he was running.

"I'm running this race, and it would be great to, you know, win it," Taylor said. It was an honest answer, even if it wasn't the whole truth.

"Maybe you want to do something else today," the man said, still looking out over the river, or the slew, or whatever it was.

"You mean like fishing?" Taylor asked, sensing that this was a kind old man inviting a visitor to fish. Maybe this riverbank was his hangout. Maybe it was like his own front porch, and WRYB was doing the neighborly thing by inviting Taylor to take a seat, the same way that Flossie would. He actually wished he had time to do it.

"Fishin's always great, but I mean what YOU really want to do today," WRYB answered.

Taylor, for some reason, felt free to answer with the complete truth. "There are a lot of things I want to do, but they can't be done in a day. I guess they're just teenager problems."

The man chuckled. "Just 'cause yo' a teenager don'

mean yo' problems aren't real."

"Thank you," Taylor said, sincerely. Ol' WRYB here seemed to understand him pretty well.

WRYB turned his head slightly to speak again, but Taylor still couldn't see his face clearly. "I think there's something else you want to do today, if you could do anything."

"What's that?"

"You want the world to see you, 'cause yo' big."

Taylor was confused. That didn't make any sense. Maybe he didn't hear WRYB correctly.

"What was that?" Taylor asked politely.

"You done heard me, son," he replied with another chuckle. WRYB liked to laugh and talk at the same time. The laugh had the sound of mischief, but maybe also the sound of wisdom.

"WRYB, you probably can't see me in this fog. I'm kind of small." This time Taylor also laughed while he talked.

He wanted to walk closer, so WRYB could see how small he was, but for some reason, his feet wouldn't move any closer.

"Naw, son," WRYB answered. "You're one of da' biggest people I've ever met. You jes' don't know it."

Taylor laughed again. "Well if I'm big, you're right

because I sure don't know it. Neither does anyone else who has ever seen me."

The laugh came again. "Son, ya' don' know what big is at all. But you will. If you decide to be big, it will change yo' life."

Taylor was riveted. "How do I decide to be big?"

"Son, I think you jes' did."

"So I'm big?" Taylor asked.

"Yep," WRYB replied, again with that chuckle.

"So what do I do now?"

"Git back on yo' path. Yo' own path, and be big."

Taylor didn't understand why, but while WRYB's words seemed as unclear as the foggy riverbank, somehow, they made sense.

"Is the crowd of runners coming? They should be here by now." Taylor wasn't sure why he expected WRYB to know the answer, but his new friend seemed to know everything.

"They're on the path for *them*, and *you* are on the path for you," he answered.

"Thank you," Taylor said.

"Son, go be big. It'll change yo' life."

"Yes, sir," Taylor replied gratefully.

"And son."

"Yes?"

"Those fellas on dat bench, they're just tryin' to impress yo' aunt. Don' believe half of what they say."

Chills ran up Taylor's arms. "Yes, sir," he replied, and sprinted off into the woods. As soon as his feet sped away, his path became clear. Maybe more than one path had become clear.

Chapter 6

Much more than ten minutes had passed, and the tall kid could no longer see his knees because they had joined his feet beneath the rising quicksand.

And now, the approaching rustle in the thickness of the riverside woods probably meant that an animal was headed straight for him. And it sounded like a large animal.

He knew there were panthers near the Mississippi River. They migrated northward from the swamps of Louisiana, near where the river emptied into the Gulf of Mexico. The closer you got to Louisiana, the more panthers there were.

He also knew that Coahoma County, North of Greenville, was named for the red panthers that were so plentiful back in the 1800s. Coahoma meant "red panther" in the Choctaw dialect. And because that was North of here, that meant that there were more panthers here than up there because Greenville was closer to Louisiana.

He was trying to decide whether to duck his head under the quicksand to hide from the panther, but would that mean certain death? It really wasn't a great choice either way. He would first try to be perfectly still and hope the panther wouldn't notice. Fat chance, he thought. He was ducking his head. Quicksand would be a horrible way to go, but it wouldn't be as bad as a panther attack. Or would it?

Then the trees began to move, and he froze as he waited for it to appear. Whatever it was, it was sprinting, not creeping, through the woods. Maybe it was chasing something else, he hoped.

That was when it appeared. Of all the things in this forest, it was the one he had least expected to see.

There he was. It was the short kid, the refugee from Refuge, Mississippi, whatever his name was. Suddenly, he wished he had learned the little runt's name.

"Hey," he called out. "I know you don't like me, but would you mind going to get help? Or throw me a stick, or something?"

Taylor didn't miss the fact that the guy didn't know his name, but that didn't matter. This was life or death, and the poor guy was terrified.

Taylor glanced around, and then tried to yank some tree limbs. Everything was either too large to break off from the tree or too small to help save him. The only things he could find in abundance were those thick vines that would do more harm than good.

Or would they?

"I'll throw you a vine and pull while you use the vine to climb out," Taylor said.

To his surprise, the tall guy shook his head. "Can't do it. My arms are too tired. And there's no leverage for my legs."

Taylor suddenly had an idea. It was kind of crazy, but it was maybe the guy's only chance unless a big crowd arrived to save him, and that didn't look likely.

Taylor pulled off all the vines he could in about one minute. The tall guy was almost waist deep in the quicksand, and the speed of his sinking seemed to increase.

The vine was thankfully really long. Taylor bent it half-way, making a two-threaded, thicker vine. It was about fifteen yards long after he doubled it. Wrapping one end around an old, sturdy tree, he wrapped the other end around his waist and tied it with a double knot. The tall kid watched, helplessly, wondering what Taylor was doing.

"My chest!" The tall kid exclaimed. Taylor looked over at him and realized that his entire chest had sunk below the surface of the quicksand. There was now no doubt that this guy had entered full-panic mode.

Taylor pulled on the vine to make sure it was wrapped firmly around the tree.

"Please hurry!" The poor guy was half-screaming, half-pleading with Taylor. The desperate voice now shook with fear.

Then Taylor pulled on the double-knot around his waist. Then he ran three long steps and jumped into the air, landing in the quicksand. While in the air, he reached out, and the tall kid understood to grab his arm.

So there they were, the two of them, in the quicksand. There was no time to talk. Taylor began pulling on the rope while the tall guy held on to his shoulders. The first couple of yanks didn't help, and Taylor was close to joining his friend in panic, but the third pull brought a result. They moved about a foot. It wasn't a lot, but it was movement. So he pulled again. And he pulled again.

Taylor spotted a tree root almost at the edge of the quicksand. That became his goal. If he could pull them there, they could use the large, partially-above-ground root to climb out.

And that was exactly what happened. When they reached it, Taylor grabbed the root and pulled. His arms seemed too tired, but he found the energy. When he was partially out, he twisted to allow the tall kid to grab the root as well. They were safe now.

They had stopped to breathe for a moment before climbing out when they heard the sound of the approaching crowd.

Rescue workers, some forestry men and women, and medical workers emerged first from the woods. Dozens of families were right behind them. Taylor's Dad had come to help, having no idea that his son was involved. Taylor was glad he was on the shore before his Dad arrived so he wouldn't have to see his son in danger.

"Do you have any medical issues?" A nurse asked as the medical people began to check for problems.

"Yes, I got stuck in quicksand," Taylor replied, and the nurse and the entire crowd laughed. That seemed to change the mood of the crowd from fear to relief.

Everyone gathered closer, hoping to hear what was being said and learn what had happened.

When the lead rescue worker asked them to describe what had happened, Taylor looked at the other guy. To Taylor's surprise, the tall guy spoke first when they asked what happened. He explained how Taylor risked his own life to save the life of someone he didn't know.

The crowd broke into a loud applause. The crowd parted to give the guys room to walk. Taylor's Dad walked with him, hand on his son's quicksand-covered shoulder.

"You came up big today," his Dad said.

"Big?" Taylor asked, surprised at the use of the word.

"Yes, big." His Dad replied. "I can't imagine a bigger need for courage at your age than you just showed. So what were you thinking while you saved his life?"

"I really wasn't thinking," Taylor admitted. "It just happened."

"Nobody can ever call you small again," said his Dad.

After all the explaining, the tears, the celebrations, and his thanking everyone for the nice things they said about him, the day got even better when Aunt Flossie's gumbo won the blue ribbon.

At first, Taylor wondered if they were giving it to his family because of the quicksand rescue, but then he learned that the judges did a blind taste-test to rate the different gumbo entries. Lem's family won an honorable mention ribbon for their Lebanese gumbo, which was cool.

Everyone ate gumbo and hung out, the final part of the festival before the Delta blues band was scheduled to begin their performance. Thankfully, Taylor's mom had packed extra clothes in case he wanted to change after the Run for the Melting Pot. The four teenagers hung out together, Taylor, Lem, Clinton (the tall guy) and Woody (the short guy). They talked about stuff, just the stuff that teenagers talk about when nobody cares where the others are from. Taylor had now made three new friends.

Actually, he had made four new friends. He needed to tell Aunt Flossie that he had met her friend WRYB, who somehow knew that he was related to Flossie, and that

Clovis and Jackson were flirting with her.

He decided to wait and share that after the festival, when they returned home.

After the gumbo dinner ended and the band was tuning up, Taylor and his family walked toward their car. This time, his Dad didn't need oven mitts because Aunt Flossie's pot of gumbo was completely empty.

Once again, they passed by the bait shop. Once again, Clovis and Jackson sat on the ancient wooden bench.

"There she is, the gumbo champion of the world," announced Clovis. "If they had given a most beautiful woman trophy, you would have won that too!"

"Hey!" Jackson exclaimed. "You stole that!" He looked at Flossie. "I told Clovis I was going to say that, and he stole it."

"Did not," Clovis said, as he winked at Taylor.

Everybody laughed.

"So when will you invite your favorite people over for some championship gumbo?" Jackson asked.

"We'll see," Flossie replied, playing her hard-to-get part of the flirtation game.

"And congratulations to our hero who came up bigger than big today!" Clovis said.

Taylor stepped over to high-five them both. Jackson grabbed his hand for a brief second to get his attention and said quietly, "And remember what you were don' told, don' believe half of what you hear from us."

Taylor smiled and nodded.

As they approached the vehicle, Taylor mentioned to Flossie that he had met her friend WRYB.

Flossie stopped abruptly. "You met WRYB? Child, that's not funny."

"What do you mean?"

"I don't know what you heard, but don't believe it. That's just a legend. People been talking about some WRYB character in the fog. Fishing on some slew, night and day, never leaving. I heard that story years ago and they're still telling it. You really shouldn't listen to Clovis and Jackson. They're fun, but don't believe anything they tell you."

Taylor was at a loss for words. He decided not to mention it again to Aunt Flossie. But Jackson and Clovis knew. Maybe he would have to wait until they visited again, but he would ask them. He would learn the truth about his life-changing friend.

Two days later, during the entire drive home, Taylor had a change of plans. He originally had planned to tell the story to strategially chosen people who knew most of the prettiest girls at school. That way, the girls would ask him to tell the story.

But his many hours to think during the car ride changed that. He didn't have to trumpet his own success. He didn't care whether anyone knew. The community of Refuge had declared it Taylor Day on the day after the festival in his honor. The Volunteer Fire Department had made him an honorary lifetime member. Clinton, the tall kid, had invited him over to hang out, which he and Lem did. Clinton's Mom wept when she hugged and thanked him again for saving her son. So did his Dad.

As their vehicle entered their neighborhood, Taylor understood that he had been thanked too much already. He was big, no matter how he looked. He was big because he had decided to be big, just like WRYB had told him.

Chapter 7

Cars lined the street on the block they lived on. Taylor's first thought was that someone might have passed away. He couldn't think of anyone in bad health. He hoped it wasn't some type of accident.

Then, he saw a crowd in a yard. It was their yard. They pulled into their own driveway. Taylor saw three local television crews, some other media types, and a table set up by a radio station offering free souvenirs and a drawing for some type of prize.

His parents turned and grinned at him. Then, he realized what had happened.

"How did they find out?" Taylor asked.

"The Greenville media began calling media here to let them know," his Mom said. "They wanted to make sure your hometown understood what a big hero you are."

There was that word again: BIG. Taylor might never tire of hearing it.

And so it began, the media interviews and the congratulatory high-fives and slaps on the back. The mayor declared it Taylor Day, his second honor in a few days. He over-heard neighbors telling reporters how they always knew Taylor would become famous. It was just a matter of time.

Taylor noticed Keith, the neighborhood bully, and walked straight toward him.

The crowd parted for him as Taylor walked straight toward the big bully. Keith sported a menacing smile, but that smile faded as Taylor continued straight at him. Keith glanced around, trying to figure out whether adults in the crowd would notice that the hero was about to confront him. Keith was unaware that his minions were embarrassed by the scene, and it hadn't even start-ed.

As he walked toward the bully, Taylor muttered si-lently to himself, "Be big because you ARE big."

Keith was determined to seize control of the situa-tion, so he spoke first, as Taylor still approached him. "Welcome home, Mr. Hero! So did you walk around barefoot with your Mississippi cousins? Did you marry one of them?"

Keith expected to hear the laughter from his min-ions, who laughed at all of his jokes. Not this time. Not a sound.

But Keith did not control this scene. Taylor spoke first. "Keith, I've got something to tell you."

"You wanna do this here?" Keith was now genuinely surprised. Maybe the little punk wanted Keith to kick his tail so the television news cameras would film it. Then after beating up the Punk, he would get arrested. Maybe that was the plan.

"Right here, right now," Taylor replied with an intensity none of the other kids had ever seen.

"Ok, bring it, Punk." No matter the consequences, Keith could not back down.

Taylor walked right up to Keith's face. Keith, expecting the obvious attack, turned his body sideways to avoid the first punch and then to throw his own reply punch. Or maybe it would be a kick.

Taylor's next move was the last thing Keith would have expected.

"I forgive you," Taylor said.

Nobody spoke. Not Keith, or the minions, or the small but growing crowd around them. Taylor hoped nobody was videoing this, because he didn't want anyone to think it was a show for YouTube.

"What?" Keith had heard him clearly, but this was the only word that his surprised and confused mind could produce.

"I forgive you," Taylor said again. "For everything. No hard feelings."

Keith's minions looked at Keith and each other, unsure of

how to act.

"Why?" Keith was embarrassed by his first one-sylla-ble answer and was even more embarrassed by the second one.

"Because I can," Taylor replied, still focusing on Keith and no one else, just as he had at the garbage dumpster a few days ago.

"No one has ever said that to me," Keith replied, again embarrassed because he had no control over what he was saying.

Taylor nodded. "Now, somebody has. See you around."

Taylor walked away, leaving the surprised group as they watched him return to the adoring crowd. Keith tried to wipe a tear from one eye without anyone noticing.

As the crowd began to thin, he noticed some of the Cools waiting to talk with him. He walked over and accepted their congrats and fist-pumps.

"Dude, we want to officially invite you to join the Cools. You're a walking girl-magnet now," one said. "You need to be hanging with us. You're the biggest name at school."

Those were words he had secretly longed to hear.

"Thanks guys," Taylor said. "I'll hang with you any-time, but I can't join the Cools."

"Why not?" A different guy asked.

"I'm forming my own group," Taylor replied with a friendly nod. Two of the Cools stepped sideways, getting closer to Taylor, just in case they needed to switch to a cooler group. Taylor noticed and tried not to laugh.

"So who can join?" The first Cool asked.

"Absolutely anybody," Taylor replied. "Everyone can hang out. It will be the biggest group at school."

They parted in a friendly enough way, with Taylor now the big dog in the neighborhood. But it wouldn't stop there. He had become big when he helped Clinton in that quicksand.

He realized that being big was becoming the best version of himself. The approval of the Cools didn't matter. He would hang with them sometimes because he wanted to, not because he needed to. He would be himself, which was the biggest thing of all.

MEET THE AUTHORS

The ToBoDo Arts Creators

Tom Ward is an award-winning journalist and ghost-writer who has served as editor-in-chief of four newspapers. His published books include the best-selling novel, *I Died and Went to Mississippi,* and the Alabama Bicentennial book that was distributed by the Alabama Department of Archives and History. Tom holds a Master's in International Affairs from King's College London and Law and History degrees from The University of Alabama.

Dodd I. Ferrelle is a singer-songwriter, children's book author and Mayor of the City of Winterville, Georgia. He released nine critically acclaimed albums as a solo artist and a member of the bands *Me'an Mills, Rags,* the *Tinfoil Stars* and the *Wintervillains.* He co-authored *If You Were A Jellybean* with his artist wife, Cameron Bliss, which became a Georgia Writer's Association nominee for children's book of the year. Ferrelle has been Mayor of the City of Winterville, Georgia for nine years and continues to create music, books and screenplays.

Bowen Craig is a writer and founder of Bilbo Books Publishing. He is proud of his local art site, *Athens Uncharted* (run with co-founder Mark Katzman) and his rant site *Heretic Picayune* (with co-founder Dr. Alice Rose). He has written theatrical, radio and film pieces, and was given permission from the only remaining living writers to Americanize the WWI parody *Oh, What a Lovely War!* His books include *Keeping Away from the Joneses, Pass the Oxtail Before the World Ends* and *Hitchhiking with Salmon*.

79

9 798990 002821